Why Noah Chose the Dove

Isaac Bashevis Singer

Why Noah Chose the Dove
Pictures by Eric Carle

Translated by Elizabeth Shub

SQUARE
FISH

Farrar Straus Giroux
New York

When the people sinned and God decided to punish them by sending the flood, all the animals gathered around Noah's ark. Noah was a righteous man, and God had told him how to save himself and his family by building an ark that would float and shelter them when the waters rose.

The animals had heard a rumor that Noah was to take with him on the ark only the best of all the living creatures. So the animals came and vied with one another, each boasting about its own virtues and whenever possible belittling the merits of others.

The lion roared: "I am
the strongest of all the
beasts, and I surely must be saved."
The elephant blared:
"I am the largest. I have the
longest trunk, the biggest ears,
and the heaviest feet."

"To be big and heavy
is not so important,"
yapped the fox. "I,
the fox, am the cleverest
of all."

"What about me?"
brayed the donkey.
"I thought I was the
cleverest."

"It seems anyone can
be clever," yipped the
skunk. "I smell the best
of all the animals. My
perfume is famous."

"All of you scramble over the earth, but I'm the only one that can climb trees," shrieked the monkey.

"The only one!" growled the bear. "What do you think I do?"

"And how about me?" chattered the squirrel indignantly.

"I belong to the tiger family," purred the cat.
"I'm a cousin of the elephant," squeaked the mouse.

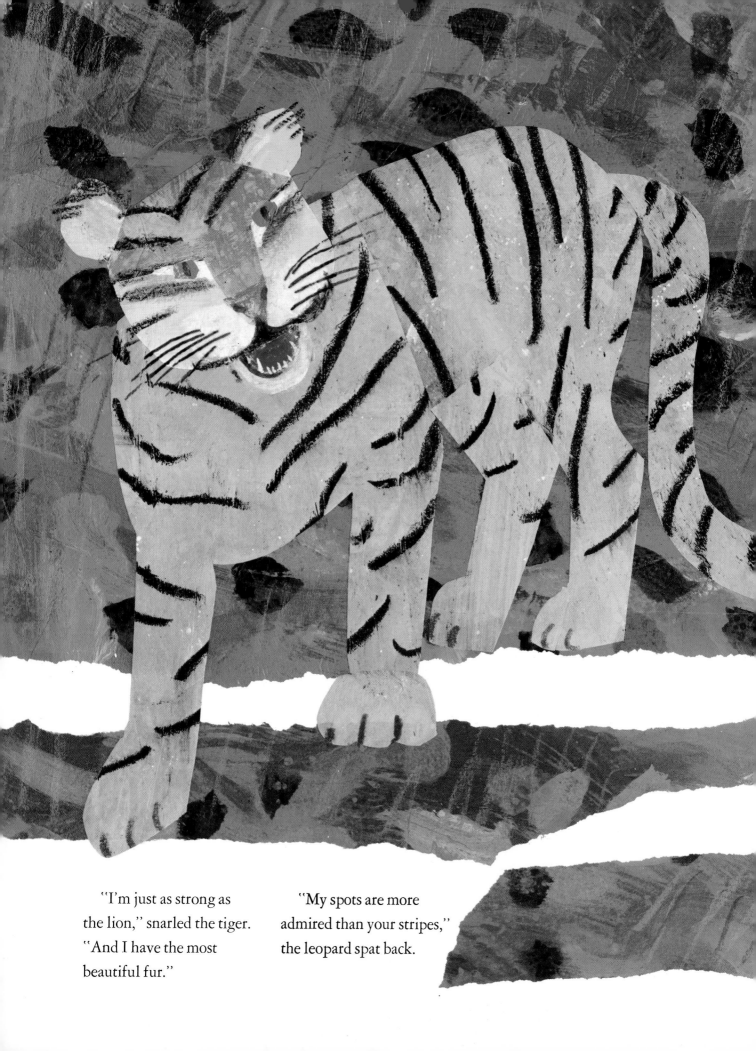

"I'm just as strong as the lion," snarled the tiger. "And I have the most beautiful fur."

"My spots are more admired than your stripes," the leopard spat back.

"I am man's closest friend," yelped the dog.

"You're no friend. You're just a fawning flatterer," bayed the wolf. "I am proud. I'm a lone wolf and flatter no one."

"Baa!" blatted the sheep. "That's why you're always hungry. Give nothing, get nothing. I give man my wool, and he takes care of me."

"You give man wool, but I give him sweet honey," droned the bee. "Besides, I have venom to protect me from my enemies."

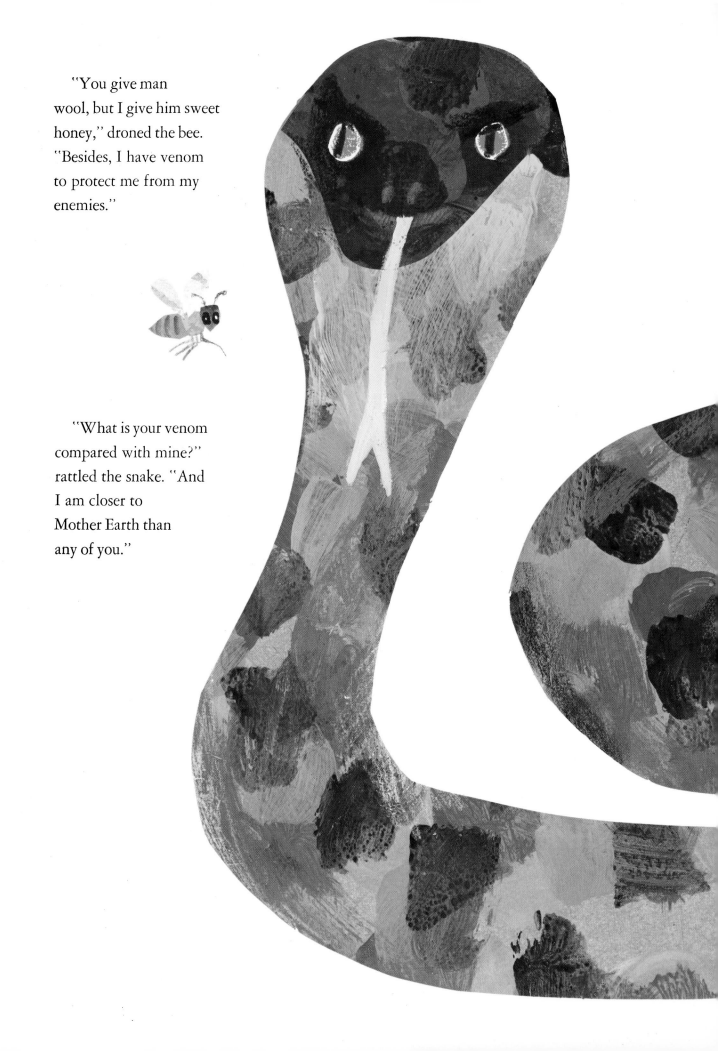

"What is your venom compared with mine?" rattled the snake. "And I am closer to Mother Earth than any of you."

"Not as close as I am," protested the earthworm, sticking its head out of the ground.

"I lay eggs," clucked the hen.

"I give milk," mooed the cow.

"I help man plow the
earth," bellowed the ox.

"I carry man," neighed the horse. "And I have the largest eyes of all of you."

"You have the largest eyes, but you have only two, while I have many," the house fly buzzed right into the horse's ear.

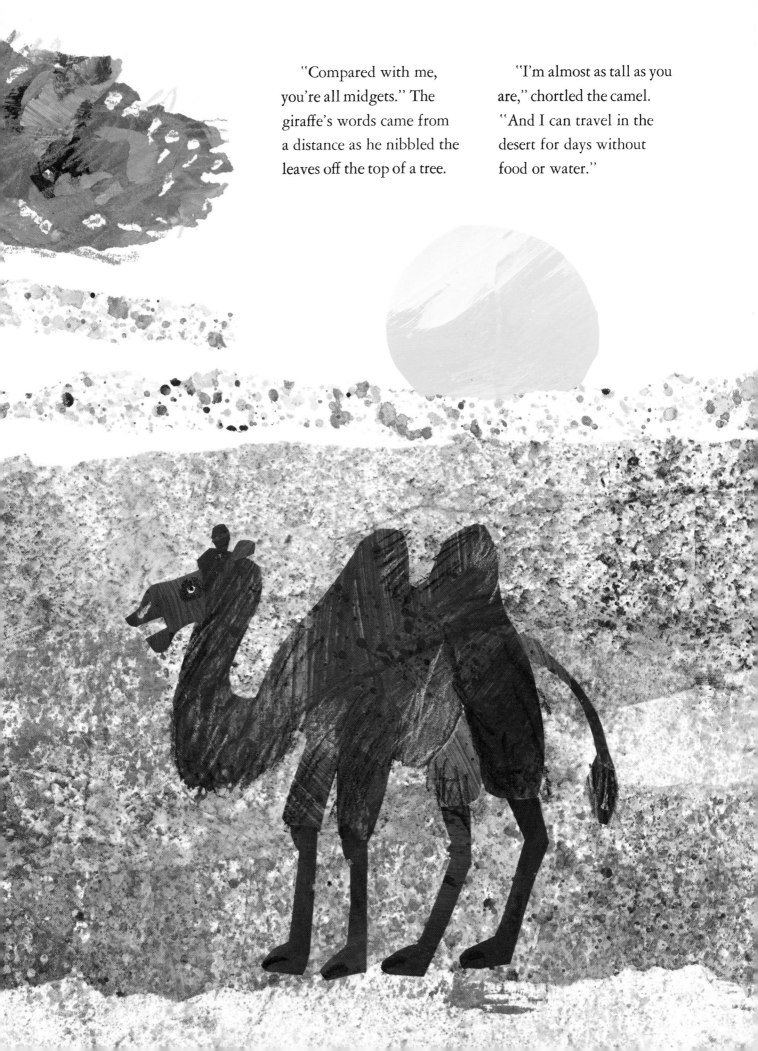

"Compared with me,
you're all midgets." The
giraffe's words came from
a distance as he nibbled the
leaves off the top of a tree.

"I'm almost as tall as you
are," chortled the camel.
"And I can travel in the
desert for days without
food or water."

"You two are tall, but I'm fat," snorted the hippopotamus. "And I'm pretty sure that my mouth is bigger than anybody's."

"Don't be so sure," snapped the crocodile, and yawned.

"I can speak like a human," squawked the parrot.

"You don't really speak. You just imitate," the rooster crowed. "I know only one word, 'cock-a-doodle-doo,' but it is my own."

"I see with my ears;
I fly by hearing," piped the bat.
"I sing with my wing,"
chirped the cricket.

There were many more creatures who were eager to praise themselves. But Noah had noticed that the dove was perched alone on a branch and did not try to speak and compete with the other animals.

"Why are you silent?" Noah asked the dove. "Don't you have anything to boast about?"

"I don't think of myself as better or wiser or more attractive than the other animals," cooed the dove. "Each one of us has something the other doesn't have, given us by God who created us all."

"The dove is right," Noah said. "There is no need to boast and compete with one another. God has ordered me to take creatures of all kinds into the ark, cattle and beast, bird and insect."

The animals were overjoyed when they heard these words, and all their grudges were forgotten.

Before Noah opened the door of the ark, he said: "I love all of you, but because the dove remained modest and silent while the rest of you bragged and argued, I choose it to be my messenger."

Noah kept his word. When the rains stopped, he sent the dove to fly over the world and bring back news of how things were. At last she returned with an olive leaf in her beak, and Noah knew that the waters had receded. When the land finally became dry, Noah and his family and all the animals left the ark.

After the flood God promised that never again would he destroy the earth because of man's sins, and that seed time and harvest, cold and heat, summer and winter, day and night would never cease.

The truth is that there are in the world more doves than there are tigers, leopards, wolves, vultures, and other ferocious beasts. The dove lives happily without fighting. It is the bird of peace.

SQUARE
FISH

An Imprint of Macmillan

Library of Congress catalog card number: 73-87426
ISBN 978-1-250-02199-1

Originally published in the United States by Farrar Straus Giroux
First Square Fish Edition: February 2013
Square Fish logo designed by Filomena Tuosto
mackids.com

2 4 6 8 10 9 7 5 3 1

AR: 3.9 / LEXILE: AD660L